The Billy Goats Gruff

Edited by Nova Nestrick • Illustrated by Barbara Remington

PLATT & MUNK, *Publishers*

NEW YORK

Other books in the Early Fun-To-Read Classics series:

THE GINGERBREAD BOY
THE TALE OF PETER RABBIT
THE LITTLE RED HEN AND THE GRAIN OF WHEAT
THE THREE LITTLE PIGS
OLD MAN RABBIT'S DINNER PARTY
THE ROOSTER, THE MOUSE AND THE LITTLE RED HEN
THE THREE BEARS AND GOLDILOCKS

O

nce

upon

a time

there lived three billy goats.

They were called

the Billy Goats Gruff.

The biggest billy goat
was Big Billy Goat Gruff.

The middle-sized billy goat
was Middle-sized
Billy Goat Gruff.

The littlest billy goat
was Little Billy Goat Gruff.

The three Billy Goats Gruff
lived in a valley.
They liked to eat
the fresh green grass
that grew in the valley.

The three Billy Goats Gruff
ate grass all day long.
They ate and ate.

At last they ate up
all the fresh green grass
in the valley.

"What shall we do?"
asked Little Billy Goat Gruff.
"There is no more
grass for us to eat
in this valley.
Where can we find
some more grass to eat?"

Big Billy Goat Gruff said,
"We will go to the hills
on the other side of the stream.
There we will find
fresh green grass to eat."

12

"Early in the morning
we will cross the stream.
We will go to the hills
and eat fresh green grass
all day long,"
said Big Billy Goat Gruff.

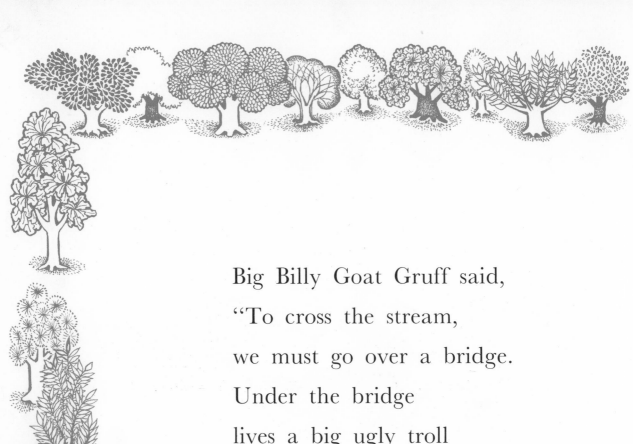

Big Billy Goat Gruff said,

"To cross the stream,

we must go over a bridge.

Under the bridge

lives a big ugly troll

with big eyes and a long nose.

He likes to eat billy goats.

And he does not like anyone

to go over his bridge.

We must be very careful."

14

Very early next morning
Little Billy Goat Gruff awoke.
He said, "I am hungry.
I will go across the bridge
to the hills, all by myself,
and eat the grass there.
I will cross the bridge
very quietly.
Then perhaps the big ugly troll
will not hear me."

Little Billy Goat Gruff started off.

Soon he came to the bridge
over the stream.

Trip trap, trip trap,

onto the bridge he went.

"Who is walking over
my bridge?" asked the big ugly troll.
"It is I," said Little Billy Goat Gruff.
"I am going to the hills
to eat grass and grow fat."

"Oh no, you are not!"
shouted the troll.
"I am coming to eat you."
"Please, Mr. Troll,
don't eat me,"
said Little Billy Goat Gruff.
"Wait for Middle-sized
Billy Goat Gruff.
He is bigger than I am."

So the big ugly troll
let Little Billy Goat Gruff
cross the bridge, trip trap.

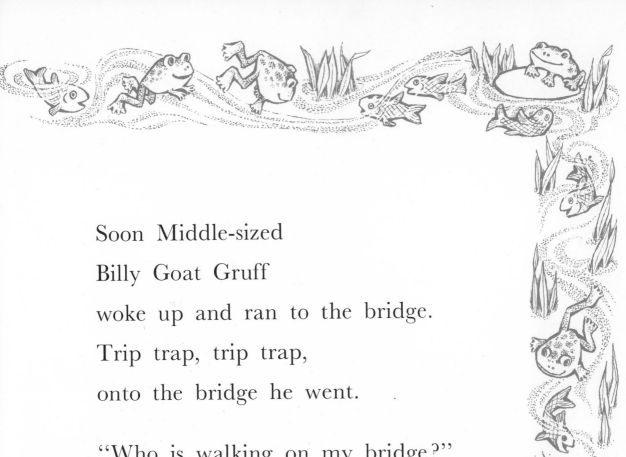

Soon Middle-sized
Billy Goat Gruff
woke up and ran to the bridge.
Trip trap, trip trap,
onto the bridge he went.

"Who is walking on my bridge?"
shouted the troll.
"I am Middle-sized
Billy Goat Gruff.
I am going to the hills
on the other side of the bridge
to eat grass and grow fat."

The big ugly troll said
in a big loud voice,
"Oh no, you are not going
to cross the bridge.
I am coming to eat you."

"Oh please don't eat me,"
said Middle-sized
Billy Goat Gruff.
"Wait for Big Billy Goat Gruff.
He is bigger than I am.
He will be along soon."

"Very well," said the troll.
He let Middle-sized
Billy Goat Gruff
cross the bridge, trip trap.
Then Middle-sized
Billy Goat Gruff ran off
to the hills and joined
Little Billy Goat Gruff.

"We got away from the troll,"
they said,
"And Big Billy Goat Gruff
will get away from him, too."

Soon Big Billy Goat Gruff awoke.

He did not see

the other two Billy Goats Gruff.

"They have gone to the hills

to eat grass," he said.

"I will go there, too."

Off went Big Billy Goat Gruff.

Soon he came to the bridge.

Tramp tramp, tramp tramp,

went Big Billy Goat Gruff

onto the bridge.

The big ugly troll was waiting
for Big Billy Goat Gruff.
When he heard the tramp tramp
on the bridge,
he knew it was
Big Billy Goat Gruff.

"Who is walking on my bridge?"
said the troll, just to be sure.

"IT IS I, BIG BILLY GOAT GRUFF.

I am going to cross your bridge.

I am going to the hills

to eat grass and grow fat."

"Oh no, you are not!"
said the big ugly troll.
"I am going to eat you,
and here I come!"
"Come on up," said Big
Billy Goat Gruff.
"I am not afraid of you!"

So up climbed the troll
from under the bridge.

Big Billy Goat Gruff looked
very big and strong.
But the troll said to himself,
"This big goat will be
a good meal for me."

The troll started toward him.
Big Billy Goat Gruff
put his head down
and ran at the troll.

"BUMP!" went Big Billy Goat Gruff.
"SPLASH!" went the troll in the water.

Then Big Billy Goat Gruff joined
the other two Billy Goats Gruff
in the hills.
They ate grass and grew fat,
and lived happily ever after.